LG-2.0-0.5 pts

PICK A PUMPKIN, MRS. MILLIE!

by Judy Cox

illustrated by Joe Mathieu

Marshall Cavendish Children

Marshall Cavendish Corporation
99 White Plains Road, Tarrytown, NY 10591
www.marshallcavendish.us/kids

Library of Congress Cataloging-in-Publication Data
Cox, Judy.
  Pick a pumpkin, Mrs. Millie! / by Judy Cox; illustrated
by Joe Mathieu.
    p. cm.
  Summary: Silly teacher Mrs. Millie gets her words
wrong when the class goes on a field trip to a pumpkin
patch.
  ISBN 978-0-7614-5573-8
  [1. Teachers—Fiction. 2. School field trips—Fiction.
3. Humorous stories.] I. Mathieu, Joseph, ill. II. Title.
  PZ7.C83835Pi 2009
  [E]—dc22
  2008029401

The illustrations are rendered
in Prismacolor pencil, dyes, pen, and ink.
Book design by Vera Soki
Editor: Margery Cuyler

Printed in Malaysia
First edition
1 3 5 6 4 2

Marshall Cavendish
Children

For Farmer Don
—J.C.

To Bella, Slone, and Joe with love
—J.M.

Mrs. Millie, our teacher, is really silly.
"Good morning, class!" she says. "It's *mice* to see you!"
"It's nice to see you, too, Mrs. Millie!" we say.

"Today we are going to the pumpkin *pets*," Mrs. Millie tells us.

"Don't be silly, Mrs. Millie! You mean the pumpkin patch!"

"We'll pick pumpkins for our Harvest Party
and bring them *yak* to school."
"No!" we shout. "You mean back to school!"

We line up to get on the bus. "It's cold today,"
Mrs. Millie says. "Don't forget your *jackals*!"
"Don't you mean our jackets?" we ask, giggling.

At the farm, Farmer Don greets us at the gate.
"We'll go on a hayride," says Mrs. Millie.
"Everybody on the *dragon*!"
"Don't be silly, Mrs. Millie! You mean the wagon!"

The hayride takes us down the road. "Look!"
calls Mrs. Millie. "A *harecrow*!"
"We know what you mean—a scarecrow!"
we tell her.

We climb off the wagon and run into the field. "Be sure to pick a *pig* one!" calls Mrs. Millie.
"Mrs. Millie! You mean a big one!"

We wade through the muddy field.
"Look for round, orange *pumas*!" calls Mrs. Millie.
"Pumpkins!" we shout.

After everyone has found a pumpkin, we load them onto the wagon. "Now we will visit the barn," says Mrs. Millie. "You can *bee* the animals."

"Don't be silly, Mrs. Millie! You mean see the animals!"

We feed the horses. We toss grain to the chickens. Mrs. Millie takes a picture of the pigs. "Time to pet the *boats*!" she says, smiling.

"Silly Mrs. Millie, you mean the goats!"

Mrs. Millie pets a billy.

"Let's help Farmer Don *snake* the leaves," says Mrs. Millie.

"You're so silly!" we cry. "You mean rake the leaves." We jump into the leaf pile.

"I spy a corn maze!" says Mrs. Millie. "Who wants
to play hide and *sheep*?"

"Hide and seek, Mrs. Millie!" we yell.

"Ready for some hot apple *spider*?" asks Mrs. Millie.

"You mean apple cider!" we say. "How can you be so silly?"

Finally it's time to leave. "We'll take our pumpkins back to *mule*," says Mrs. Millie.

"We know what you mean—back to school!" we shout.

"We can carve them into *gecko*'-lanterns!"
"Silly Mrs. Millie! You mean jack-o'-lanterns!"
we tell her.

"Wasn't the pumpkin patch *fawn*?" Mrs. Millie says as we line up for the bus.

"Yes, Mrs. Millie, we had fun!" we shout.

Farmer Don loads our pumpkins onto the bus.

"Thank you!" we tell him.

As the bus pulls away, we wave good-bye to Farmer Don and his billy *boats*.